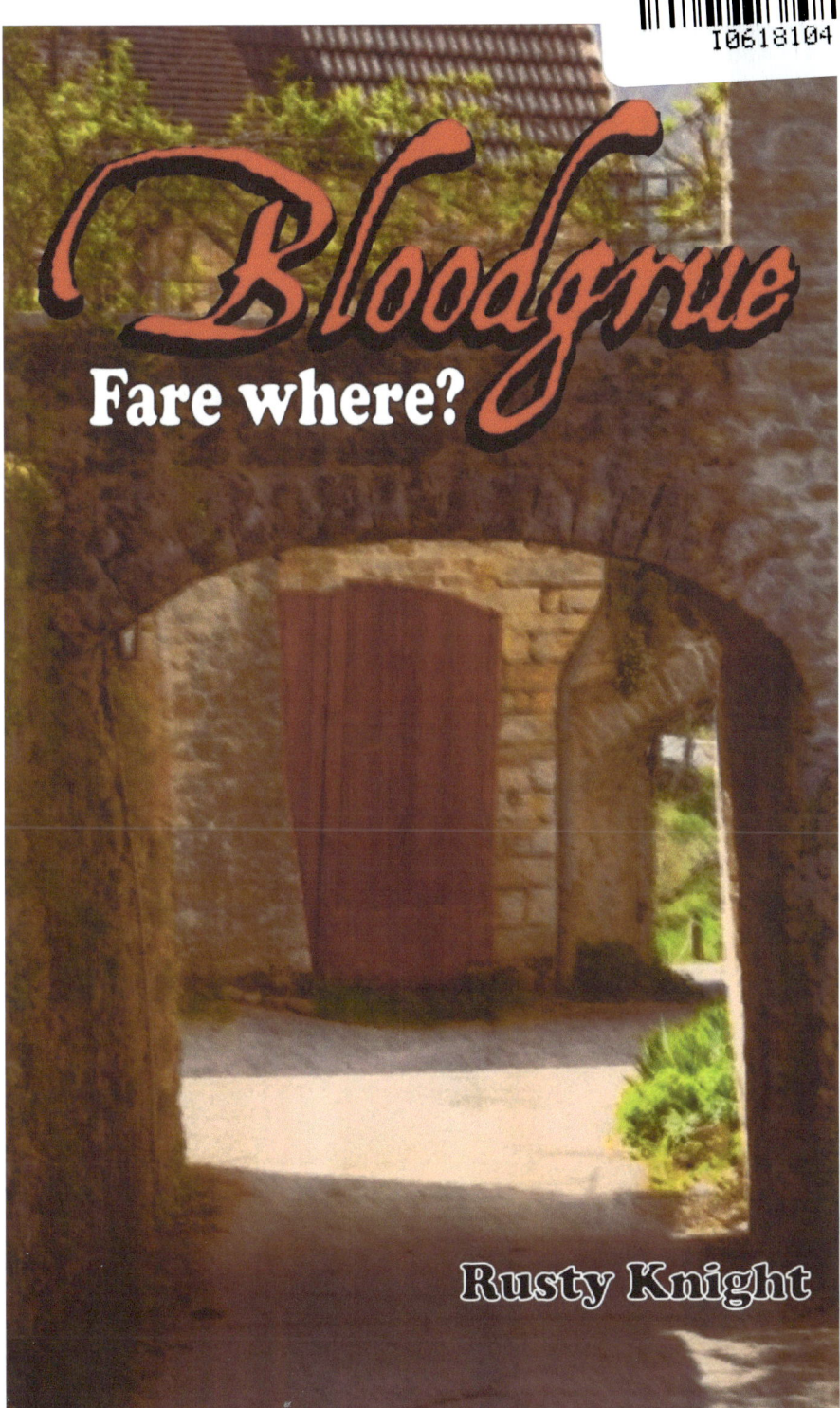

Bloodgrue

Fare where?

Rusty Knight

Welcome to our serial stories!

If you're not familiar with our serial series, think of them as a favorite nighttime program that continues with a new episode each story, only in a print format. These are stories that don't necessarily have an end planned for them, or if they do, it's a long way off unlike many television series we get interested in only to have them go off air.

Serial stories are a great way to keep you entertained and on edge waiting to see what will happen next in short enough episodes to enjoy on a lunch break or before going to bed. Although our stories are designed to be read one episode per week, unlike TV stories, if you just can't wait for the next episode, you can get these any time.

Please feel free to let us know what you think of our serial stories. It's a trend that may take some getting used to, but we've had positive feedback in the past with them.

Now, it's time to enjoy!

Thank you from InUPress & Rusty Knight

We would like to acknowledge the following for their work in the production of this series.

The cover design is by, C S Burgar

The editing is by, Donna Shumaker (Aria)

Autumn 76 Lizard, *King Dolan IV has just been coroneted and we are meeting Bloodgrue, who is in his fourth year of dragoman apprenticeship with his master, Journeyman Dragoman Onar. Bloodgrue is hampered and aided by many foes and friends in the North Docks district, District 5 of the royal city of Mount Oryn. Onar supplies Bloodgrue with one meal a day, if Bloodgrue brings home coin from any source.*

We learn how Bloodgrue and his friend Noah work together. In his work, Bloodgrue meets up with another companion, The Fellow, a hunter. In frustration Bloodgrue meets Luenen and the rogue guild, Pandora. Bloodgrue becomes deeply infatuated with Lena, a master carpenter's daughter. During this time Bloodgrue fends off the advances of journeyman brick-maker, Lilla.

Bloodgrue
By Rusty Knight
Episode One, 'Bloodgrue'

Autumn 76 Lizard: The sphere is clear as the gods breathe strongly eastward. Bloodgrue watches the skinny, armoured jalmal who is seeking help. The tall, unattractive, seventyish appearing man seems lost. So, Bloodgrue does his job. He approaches the man hoping, as usual, that the jalmal speaks native jalnoric. Sometimes they don't; rarely, but sometimes.

In clear jalnoric speech, Bloodgrue offers the man, "Hello outter, you look lost. I am a dragoman apprentice. Perhaps I can help you. My name is Bloodgrue."

Drawing back slightly for a moment, looking down at the urchin who approached him, Genner thinks about the offer. "Yes! Yes, I need help. I am here for the coronation of the new king. My barge was late so I missed the ceremonies, but I am still going to Palace Hill to grant tribute. Who around here can guide me to the Palace, or to a place near the palace I can stay? I am Sir Genner Mal."

A particularly strong gust of breath ruffles clothing and dust, irritating those it passes. Bloodgrue blinks the dryness away from his eyes, then answers. "Sir Genner, I can escort you to near the palace easy enough. It will cost you one Dyns a day, plus food and lodging. Fair enough? We can start right away. Do you have others to go with you?"

Genner guffaws and shifts uneasily for a moment or two as he looks about, watching the crowded dock. North Dock's citizens are an odd mix, as all classes of society mingle here. Lower, middle and upper class mingle shoulder to shoulder together. Sir Genner is a knight, though he is not a landed knight, so he is not upper-class as such. But still, he is a knight so he is upper-middle-class.

Bloodgrue is dressed in near rags, which indicates lower-class. At best his clothing suggests upper-lower-class, even though the dragomen are actually middle-class. So to Genner this is confusing. In Genner's mind this makes Bloodgrue a very

poor lower-middle-class, which indicates his master is either not very successful, or he is a very deep miser.

Sir Genner is a river sailor, when not being a knight, so he knows appearances can be deceiving and thus he comes to a harsh decision. "I will hire you. But you keep two paces to the side. If I feel you are misguiding me or are being inappropriate, I will report you, or deal with you myself. The best you can hope for is firing with full pay, if I have to deal with you myself. Understood Bloodgrue?"

Bloodgrue bows politely as he understands his appearance throws folks off. Master Onar refuses to buy upgraded clothing for Bloodgrue, never mind supplying more than one meal a day. If Bloodgrue does not get one client in a day, Onar doesn't even feed Bloodgrue. So Bloodgrue bows then offers his arm in the customary arm clasp to seal an agreement. He is happy that Genner never took to renegotiating fees.

"Sir Genner, I take it you came in on a barge. Do you have baggage? Which barge do we need to unload you from?"

Sir Genner, concluding Bloodgrue knows deal etiquette, accepts the arm clasp and seals the deal. Responding casually to Bloodgrue's questions, Sir Genner answers cautiously. "I sailed in on the Hawk's Nose as its 1st mate. I have no baggage, apprentice. Let us begin our journey. The gods rose half an hour ago, so if we get moving we can make some good distance. If you want to jabber, we can do it while we walk."

Bloodgrue smiles and with a shallow bow, he acknowledges the command. "Follow me Sir Genner."

Bloodgrue leads the way silently up the slopes of the river dock's bank of streets to Osmo Road, navigating the crowd for the pair. He keeps his two pace distance as requested by Sir Genner.

Finally, reaching Osmo Road, Bloodgrue stops and watches the traffic as Sir Genner recuperates from the jostling of the dock's streets. In his mind, Bloodgrue plans out their route.

"I think we will head toward Oak Street, but before walking Oak Street we will turn south onto Willow Road. We will follow Willow Road down into Velan District which is District four, that will then bring you closer to the Palace districts and Palace Hill. We can stay overnight in the Nobleman's Inn and continue on in the morning from there. I feel from the pace we might set; it will be near the time of gods-set when we reach Nobleman's. There is a closer inn, the Willow Rest, but we can gain four hours on the journey tomorrow by continuing to the Nobleman's today. What do you say Sir Genner?"

Sir Genner, frowning, thinks a while on this, then nodding he answers curtly. "Let's make it to the Nobleman's Inn tonight. Start walking boy."

Bloodgrue turns east to start on the journey.

Bloodgrue considers what he has with him: worn old cloth shoes, a tunic that is almost see-through and needs washing, leggings that are four years old, his only pair and need patching, a cloth belt holding his leggings on, a small cloth pouch attached to the belt which contains his worldly possessions; three copper dusters and a small rust pitted knife with a 2-inch blade. Oh yes, also a small green ball that is seven feet of 1/8-inch jute twine. This is all Bloodgrue has to show for being an apprentice, since his twelfth birthday, with Master Dragoman Onar. Bloodgrue turned sixteen, last Spring 12 Unicorn. It was sad, as he was alone that day, and try as he might he couldn't acquire a client. So, he went to sleep without a meal on his sixteenth birthday! There were no friends to celebrate his birthday with him, but he wasn't feeling particularly like celebrating. Right now, though, he could celebrate, as this is the perfect job, as it should be at least four days in length. This job should pay four Dyns. He should get to sleep on a cot, at worst, for four nights, instead of on the floor of his furniture-less eight-foot by ten-foot room.

Plus, he will be fed, so how could he not want to celebrate? He gets one of these jobs every couple of seasons.

The pair turns down Willow Road, still observing the silence Genner instilled upon their journey.

This road has traffic going both directions. Bloodgrue, being polite, observes his client's demands, it is just that sometimes he needs to communicate with anyone who will communicate back. Bloodgrue has had enough silence; he has to try having conversation at least once this trip. "It's odd to me how we have to start a whole new calendar because we have a new King. What was wrong with the old calendar? We couldn't continue with the year of the Unicorn when King Dolan the IV was coroneted today? We have to get rid of the old calendars today and officially start new calendars at year of the Lizard? So today doesn't go on the Royal Records as Autumn 76 Unicorn, 17th Cycle of King Regeanus III. It is Autumn 76 Lizard, 1st Cycle of King Dolan IV. Why couldn't we just say it is Autumn 76 Unicorn?"

"Don't ask silly questions boy. We can't continue marking time in the name of the old monarch. We have to record time in the name of the new monarch, so we start the calendar at the beginning of the cycle and the cycle starts at the year of the Lizard, then follows through the seven years of the cycle as has been done for about a thousand years. There is the reason for doing it this way."

Bloodgrue, interested in learning, is ever curious, and having Genner talking now, continues. "But why? Why do we do it this way?"

Sir Genner huffs grumpily. "How should I know? I am not a scholar or such. I sail and I hurt people. That is what I do, now shut up and keep walking or I will choose to do one of those two. We are on dry land now so you can understand which I will choose."

Bloodgrue, not the slowest fish in the river, shuts up, keeping his two pace distance from Sir Genner, as they walk along Willow Road.

After sometime they arrive near Willow Rest. There are about seven hours of gods-light left in the day. "Sir Genner, that is Willow Rest. We can stop there or keep going to the Nobleman's Inn. At this pace it will be close to dark when we arrive. It is your choice. There is nothing in-between these two." Bloodgrue stops in front of a stone and wood building, which is two stories high, that is painted brown and orange. The large sign out front has a simple, solid red square painted on it.

Sir Genner looks at the building a few moments, as he rests from their five hours of walking, then he shrugs and turns to Bloodgrue. "We go onward boy. You can still lead the way. But first we eat and you can exercise your lungs and jaw during this time. I just like to travel in quiet, but I will socialize while we feast. Is the eats good here?"

Bloodgrue sighs happily. It was yesterday morning the last time he had food. "Yes, the food is edible here. The dark ale is a winner as well."

"Then in we go boy."

Together, the pair enters the dim interior of Willow Rest. Sir Genner chooses to sit at the table near the door and wall. When the barman arrives, Sir Genner speaks up. "We will have two hot meals and two dark ales. Also, I need water for my dragoman, as he needs to talk and his speech was cracking on him last time he spoke. Bring the water right away. Bring the ales next, then the food when it's ready. Where do you keep your privy? I haven't stopped since the river."

"The privy, Sir, is back in the stable's courtyard. I will get the rest as soon as I see three Dyns."

Sir Genner chuckles as he pulls free his coin purse from his backpack. Carefully digging out three silver coins from the bulging coin purse, Sir Genner hands them to the barman. Putting the coin purse back into the backpack, Genner puts the backpack against the wall next to their table. "You stay here for now and keep an eye on that. If anything goes missing, you will be missing and not returning home. Understood?"

"Yes, Sir Genner." Stammers Bloodgrue nervously.

Sir Genner unsheathes his dagger and sets it on the table in front of Bloodgrue. "Likely you don't know how to use it, but just in case you need it. Stab with it, don't slice. I'll be right back. You best be here and my stuff be here."

Looking up at Sir Genner, Bloodgrue simply nods a nervous yes, without touching the dagger.

Looking at the dagger after Sir Genner leaves; Bloodgrue estimates it is worth to be at least two Flairs. '*I don't think Onar has anything worth two Flairs. And Genner's longsword has to be worth dozens of Flairs and his armour, I have no clue. I don't even know what kind of armour that is.*'

The barman places a mug of water on the table in front of Bloodgrue near the dagger, and offers Bloodgrue advice. "If you don't know how to use it, don't pick it up. You'll just get into more trouble than you might be able to handle, if you pick it up."

Bloodgrue eagerly drinks a few small sips of water, knowing from experience what large sips or gulps of water will do when this parched. By the time Genner returns, Bloodgrue has nursed half the mug of water and has had a few sips of the dark ale already.

Genner sits and happily sighs. "It's out back if yah need it boy. I see you're smart enough not to drain your water mug right away. Good boy."

"Sir Genner, you said I could talk now?" Asks Bloodgrue.

"Yes boy I did."

"Okay, can I ask you questions?" inquires Bloodgrue.

"Yes you may, everything, except my sex life. That doesn't exist anymore and I am not going to talk about the history of it. Go ahead." smiles Genner cantankerously.

"I don't know about weapons and armour. Or even knights and nobles. So I want to know about your armour and weapons. What type are they and what are they worth?" asks Bloodgrue eagerly.

Genner pauses for a bit as the plates of hot food are set down for the two of them. "Well, the armour is an older set of banded-mail I had made for me, at a cost of two hundred Royal Flairs, about twenty-five years ago when I was better off. Now, as to the weapons; well, the dagger you have on the table before you I picked up in my early years of training for a Flair. My short-bow, I traded three hundred pounds of salt for, six years ago. That brings us to the only weapon and armour pairing I really care to use, my longsword and knight shield. No one can defeat me while I use them. This here shield would cost over seventy Royal Flairs on the open market, if I ever was convinced to separate from it. The longsword I had specially crafted over fifty years ago and cost me one-hundred-and-fifty of those pieces of gold. A regular longsword could be fetched for fifteen. So, if you want a word of advice, don't touch my sword or shield. You won't do it twice. You can keep the dagger and learn to use it. We are also going to buy you a water-skin from here, before we continue, and fill it with the dark ale like you just finished draining."

The pair finishes eating and are on the road again. Bloodgrue, with the dagger rolled in his legging's waist band, as instructed by Genner, and a full eight-litre water-skin slung across his back, is smiling. Bloodgrue had listened and been rewarded. He hadn't been told to shut up because he wasn't wanted, but to save Bloodgrue's throat. Also, because his client likes to travel in silence, so silence is what Sir Genner gets. They travel through Willow swamp and then out into Velan District. Before the two day-gods set, the pair arrive at Nobleman's Inn. The painted Imvor-orange, wood and stone structure, stands out in the landscape, although its medium-size wooden sign with its black line drawing of a square, doesn't.

Bloodgrue turns to Sir Genner. "Are you sure? I can keep going with you. It is another full day's walk to Outer Palace Hill gates. I don't mind walking the full distance."

"No, Bloodgrue you go home. You described the roads well enough. I navigate worse sand bars. I think you earned what I gave you. You go home. I will set you up with a room and a hot meal tonight and a cold meal tomorrow at gods-rise. But that is all. You did okay. When we met I didn't trust you, but you showed me intelligence and that you can be trusted. Also, I need to travel on my own, as you talk too much. Not your fault. Some folk are that way. You do well, for about five hours of silence, but then you can't hold it in anymore. No issue, I do understand, I know many sailors the same way. You go home. Let's get in here and find rooms and food, but you only get one dark ale tonight.

That skin today might have helped loosen you up. Fill it before you leave tomorrow. I'll buy."

They enter Nobleman's Inn; Bloodgrue spots a century old jalfem wearing an apron, serving a lone customer. As she leaves the customer, Bloodgrue approaches. "Excuse me, are you the proprietor?"

She stops and appraises Bloodgrue, then Genner. Sighing, she nods. "Yes I am. This is the Nobleman's Inn. Rooms are a Dyns each a night. Hot meals are a Dyns each, dorm cots a duster. Ale is a duster a mug, it's a house brew. Waters free. There are no baths, and no laundry service."

Sir Genner coughs and steps up, quickly cutting in with his response. "I see you waste no effort, neither will we. We want two good rooms, two hot meals tonight, two more in the morning, two ales tonight, two skins full and two mugs in the morning, all for the sum of one Flair. That is my offer."

The Innkeeper, taken aback greatly, stops, looks at Genner then smiles. "Room four and five are yours. I will have your ales and meals in a minute."

Sir Genner un-slings his backpack and then digs out his coin pouch, taking a gold coin from the pouch. Genner gives the single Flair to the old crone.

The two travel companions sit down to eat and drink. "Bloodgrue, get lessons with the dagger and remember stab with it, don't try to slice. Keep it out of sight, because if someone sees it on you, they will assume you know how to use it. Always travel with a few coins and keep a full water-skin with you. It will save your life."

To be continued…

In the next episode two, *'Noah'*,

Bloodgrue goes to Western Madison to meet his best friend Noah. Noah beats a thug, robbing him. The reward enriches both friends.

Awesome! You finished an episode of '*Bloodgrue*'.

Let us know what you think of it by going to this this link: www.inupress.ca While you are there, you can join the Inevitable Unicorn Press e-mail subscription list to receive news and updates about work from our authors such as; Rusty Knight, Brian Hill and Aria. When you sign up for the e-mail list, you will receive a free pdf. This free pdf changes with time. In February 2016 the gift was a copy of Rusty Knight's biography of the protagonists, the Black Swans, from his novel, *'Laret'*. Later in 2016, the bonus was an issue from the serial series, *'Lanis'*.

While on the home page of InUPress.ca you can leave a comment telling us what you think of our author's work or about your thoughts on the website. We appreciate your time and we will respond to questions and comments.

Thank you for reading.

Yours,

Rusty Knight of Inevitable Unicorn Press.

www.inupress.ca

 *Rusty Knight* is a writer who also builds and repairs computers when he is not building blogs and web pages. Rusty Knight's writings tend towards the fantasy or sci-fi genres, but he has won an award as best new poet of the year from the American Poetry Society in the early 1980's. Rusty Knight is the lead moderator and administrator for the local writing group, Fellowship of the Scribblers.

Currently, Rusty Knight is working on a fantasy novel titled, *Laret*, due out in 2016. Rusty grew up on a mixed farm and he has the heart and soul of a self-sufficient farmer, thus he finds he is able to step into all the roles of almost every character in his world. Coming from a family of ten in a small five room house, he knows the world of no privacy, so he can relate to the world of Quantos well.

Follow *Rusty Knight* at www.inupress.ca

Please feel free to leave a review at: www.inupress.ca

Welcome to our serial stories!

If you're not familiar with our serials, think of them as a favorite nighttime program that continues with a new episode each week, only this is in a print format. These are stories that don't necessarily have an end planned for them, or if they do, it's a long way off unlike many television series that we get interested in, only to have them go off air.

Serial stories are a great way to keep you entertained and on edge waiting to see what will happen next, in short enough episodes to enjoy on a lunch break, or before going to bed. Although our stories are designed to be read one episode per week, unlike TV stories, if you just can't wait for the next episode, you can get another one any time.

Be sure to download your episodes!

It is a good idea to download the episode when you first purchase them. Then, read them at your leisure.

Please feel free to let us know what you think of our serial stories. It's a trend that may take some getting used to, but we've had positive feedback in the past with them.

Now, it's time to enjoy!

Thank you from,

Rusty Knight & InUPress

We would like to acknowledge the following for their work in the production of this series.

The cover design is by, C S Burgar

The editing is by, Donna Shumaker (Aria)

Previously in *Bloodgrue*: ***Autumn 76 Lizard****: we met the apprentice dragoman Bloodgrue. He took on a client to escort south into Velan District. The client, Sir Genner, gave Bloodgrue a dagger, as well as a couple of lessons.*

Bloodgrue
By Rusty Knight
Episode Two, 'Noah'

We continue on ...

Autumn 79 Lizard: we find Bloodgrue in the hours of darkness.

It is freezing in his barren eight-foot by ten-foot room. Bloodgrue tosses again hungrily in the corner. The souls up in the sphere are shining brightly through his un-shuttered open window. "Seven Hells, I have to move to warm up. I gotta go see Noah for something to do."

Bloodgrue bounds up onto his feet, even though the two day-gods won't rise for another hour or more. Opening his door, Bloodgrue leaves 4212 Willow Road and walks north. Then turning east onto Oak Street, at Osmo Road.

By the time Bloodgrue reaches Fifth Avenue, the two day-gods are breaking over the eastern horizon and Bloodgrue smiles. But, he waits until both gods have broken well over the horizon, and then he boldly walks fifteen paces out onto Fifth Avenue and stops. With hands in full sight he calls out loudly so all the houses on both sides can hear clearly. "I'm home honey. Where is the ale?"

Bloodgrue patiently waits, as a jalnoric to do otherwise at this point might invite death from any one of these buildings. Bloodgrue knows there are six Wardens watching from random locations in any of these eight buildings. When the Wardens think that one has sweat enough, they will acknowledge him or her. Bloodgrue knows the rules and doesn't sweat it at all. Its pride at this point to be allowed in, considering he is jalnoric and that he has a trade skill.

It is a good five minutes before two toydons, who Bloodgrue recognizes, exit the
third building on the left. Two toyfem, one is about seventeen, the other near thirty, they are armed with slings and short swords. They casually walk silently over to Bloodgrue.

Bloodgrue raises his arms level with his shoulders. "There is a dagger rolled in my waist band, but I haven't figured out how to use it yet so you're safe."

"Yah, I figure you'll do yourself more harm if you pull it, Blood. Leave it there and you can keep it in the future. Noah's down home on the south end with Wilma. They're cooking some plan to bring in merchants from Velan. I don't want to know what scheme he has now. You're clear … but play nice again. No messin' with a good thing you have here. We don't want be hurtin' you now."

All three chuckle at this. "I will leave before dark Mama. Thank you."

Bloodgrue clasps arm with both women after having answered the elders jest.

Bloodgrue boldly walks down the centre of Fifth Avenue, heading south the whole ten blocks to Noah's mom's house. It is one of the better houses, a wooden structure fairly intact with only a few damaged wooden shingles. The shutters on the few windows of the house are intact. The door is solid and only squeaks slightly. Bloodgrue once laughed, remarking how the houses in Western Madison squeaked so bad, that they were thief proof, they were already alarmed. That didn't go over so well with his audience at the time, which included three rogues and two Western Madison council members. That mistake almost got him rejected from the Ward, but they forgave him when he did three days labour for the council.

Bloodgrue knocks on the sill of the only door into the dwelling. Noah answers shortly, wearing a smile and his old clothing. "You! … What are you doing here today of all days? … I will be right out Blood."

Noah steps back inside the dark interior. "Mama, I'm headed south … like I was saying earlier. I'm taking Blood with me. I will be back in about two hours."

Wilma Nora answers her son hesitantly. "You be careful Noah; I don't like this idea at all. Those people can't be trusted in any way. And even Bloodgrue … just cause he saved you don't mean he can be trusted either. You be careful, bein sick like this, you're weaker today … so watch them jal's today."

"I'll watch them Mama ... Blood will be with me, like he is …. I know he can't help being jal, but he's my friend, so stop harpin in on him ... He can be trusted, or the Wardens wouldn't let him in like they do ... So, I'll talk to yah later Mama."

Noah comes running out the door, before his mother can send off another response to him.

Noah grabs Bloodgrue's arm on his way past Bloodgrue, whispering. "Quick or she won't shut up."

Noah is one year senior to Bloodgrue, in age, but in social rank in community, he may as well be a grandfather compared to Bloodgrue. On their walk south, Noah is greeted by everyone they pass on Fifth Avenue, as they journey towards the unofficial ward boundary.

Reaching the south boundary, they find two groups milling about. One group is the toydon destitute of Western Madison, in their rags, most are bare foot. They have no obvious methods of defense or melee, but are quite desperate looking. Opposing them are a mix of jalnoric and toydon middle-class, fewer in number, several carry knives or daggers. A couple arrived carrying clubs, one even came with a hand axe and buckler.

Bloodgrue looks around, shocked at the disparity, and to even find this situation at all. This area is a known no-man's-land, usually void of any life for the full block. Six buildings on either side are evenly claimed, three by each side. The middle-class Velan district doesn't want unchecked Western Madison citizens wandering south into Velan.

The Western Madison citizens don't trust the Velan wandering into Western Madison. So the Velan District and Western Madison ward both keep watch here.

Noah scratches some open sores on the back-side of his hand as he walks boldly forward, also making sure to drag Bloodgrue along. He stops halfway between the two groups. "Yah, hey! I am looking for Terri. The damn thug sent a message saying he had a deal to make with me, inside Western Madison."

A very short husky jalmal steps out of the pack of middle-class and he confidently walks alone towards Noah. The jalmal has a pack on his back and is armed with a knife and sling.

"I'm Terri. You think you can use that short-sword or dagger if you need?" huskily utters the muscular short jalmal.

Noah smiles and in his best jalnoric continues the conversation. "Well now I think if I need to I can handle these very well. This gentleman here is my second, his name is Bloodgrue, and he is a dragoman. My name is Noah. I think you sent a message that you have a merchant deal to make in Western Madison. I am the one you talk to, to make a deal."

The fifty-five-year-old jalmal steps back, grimly shaking his head. "You're a kid, speaking merchants tongue like a seasoned merchant. You're from Western Madison. You a thief?"

Without a verbal answer, Noah swings out with both his left arm and leg like he practiced so many times, connecting with Terri's right arm and leg, sending Terri to the ground.

Obviously you don't call Noah a thief, if you are from outside of Western Madison. Noah is apparently angry, as his face is red and his breathing has become very deep and controlled. He is breathing through his nose, with his lips very tight. Noah takes up his fighting stance as Terri regains his feet, his knife drawn, now upset, looking in shock.

Terri's eyes are wide and red, his face paler than earlier, with his breathing now erratic. Terri charges Noah, swinging at Noah with his knife as Noah deflects it while striking out with both fists.

Terri, in frustrated anger, turns back around to strike at Noah, missing Noah with a wild swing neck high.

Noah attempts to re-center himself while swinging his fist around regaining balance; he then kicks out connecting with Terri's left arm, knocking Terri flying again.

Terri shakes himself back to his senses.

Noah takes up his fighting stance yet again, ready for another go.

Terri looks at the crowd and sees no one coming to his aid. Being knocked down twice by a street punk; Terri is a known street thug with a reputation as a strong proficient fighter. He assesses that this street punk just may be able to use those weapons as well. Today is not the day to find out alone. Jumping back up on to his feet in a flash, Terri trips, and loses his pack.

Noah rushes Terri, which gives Terri incentive to run, as Bloodgrue also takes the moment to close in on Terri.

Leaving his pack, Terri joins his seventeen middle-class Velan district merchants, as thirty-eight Western Madison desperate rush forward towards the centre.

Noah holds up both hands. The West stops. Noah points back towards their ward while smiling. He picks up the pack and waves at the Velan.

Walking towards the Western, Noah says happily to Bloodgrue. "It weighs about eight pounds. I wonder how much of it is coin? Let's go to the Red Square."

The mob cheers and congratulates both Noah and Bloodgrue. Again, Noah has won accolades from his people. Noah is seventeen years old and has already been a local hero for two years. That is the only way Bloodgrue gets in to Western Madison easily, by being Noah's friend. When they were twelve and thirteen, Noah was pinned to the ground by a brute of a dog, being thrashed nearly dead. Bloodgrue had been walking nearby and saw this; he picked up a brick that was close at hand and bashed in the brains of the dog. Noah was unconscious, so Bloodgrue ran to the nearby Warden watch-post at Oak and Fifth, where he got the Wardens. He actually helped save Noah's life. The community still remembers, but with Bloodgrue being jal they don't forget that. It is an uneasy truce and balancing act for Bloodgrue, always wary about his actions in Western Madison.

Knowing that at any time, one of the two-hundred and forty-three residents could call his intentions and have him expelled permanently, no matter what he had done previously.

Today he is a hero as well, tomorrow who knows. The tempers change here as fast as the breath of the gods.

The hour walk to the Red Square is jubilant for all. Noah refrains from shaking the pack to hear it jingle, but his smile will light the tavern for days. Bloodgrue worries as Noah does look a little grey from illness now.

Sitting down at the table they chose, Bloodgrue and Noah sigh together. "Do we count it here?" asks Bloodgrue excited.

Noah unties a strap and peaks in, then slowly shakes his head. He frowns suddenly. "NO! In a room ... One moment please ... Willa, come here, please."

The barmaid strolls casually over, she smiles at the duo. "So … last time you two were in here I earned two dusters in tips ... What will it be this time?"

Noah hands her a Flair that he had palmed from the pack. "How about Blood and I have a private room to drink in? I will pay for a full day now and drinks, with a second Flair ... But the first is a tip, so keep it out of sight Sweetheart."

Willa looks at the coin, then Noah. She smiles. "Room three is all yours, boys ... What will you be drinking?"

Noah takes her hand and kisses the back of it. Releasing it, he places two more Flairs in the palm and closes her hand. "Well, actually three rounds of ale. I also would like two basins of hot water, two good towels and a set of wash cloths ... Also, could you send someone for seamstress Guilda, please Sweetheart?"

"Sure thing, Coin-a-lot, Guilda will be right here. The ales will be right in room three, as quick as I can pour them and carry them over." Stammers Willa excitedly.

The two boys stand and with Noah leading, they walk to room three. Willa stands there watching them, her hand closed tightly and she is smiling, lost in thought. There now, yet another convert for Noah's brigade of followers.

Sitting the pack on the sturdy wooden table, Noah looks around the room as Bloodgrue closes the door. In the room are four rough but sturdy chairs, the table, a chamber pot and a single un-shuttered small window. The ceiling is mere inches above their heads, and is a stuccoed brown. The pine floor is well-worn, smooth from much use, but it is clean.

Bloodgrue nods approvingly. "Okay, so you earned a day's drinking in here. Nice, then what? You made another enemy outside of Western Madison. Nice kick, by the way. You sent him flying good. You have been practicing again, haven't you? Hey, can you teach me to use a dagger?"

Noah sits down with an air of confidence as he gazes about the room. A broad smirk is on his face like he ate the best dessert that his mother ever cooked, before anyone else got a bite. He looks at Bloodgrue, waiting. "Sit down you nervous scat. We wait for Willa to bring the drinks, then I show you how big of an enemy, WE really made."

There is a knock, then the door opens and Willa enters with her tray of six ales. She professionally sets the ales on the table. Swinging the tray aside, she adds. "Guilda will be here shortly. I have a hot meal coming for both you boys, after the hot water and wash towels. Then, you will have your peace to carouse together. Don't cost me the whole tip in repairs. Okay boys?"

Noah smiles disarmingly. "Willa, if we do any damages, I will leave coins for the repairs. I promise."

Bloodgrue and Willa both drop their jaws. Then Willa hurries out closing the door behind her.

Noah unties all the catches on the pack, and then sets it on the floor beside his chair. "You want to know how profitable beating jalnoric merchants can be?"

They count out fifty-two Royal Flairs. "I gave Willa three also. So that thug brought fifty-five Flairs to buy Western Madison ward with. He wanted to buy the whole ward. Do you believe it?"

Bloodgrue is still stunned. Then suddenly he has an idea on how he might profit from this.

"Okay, tell you what, oh mighty dog food. Why don't we play a drinking game? We look each other in the eye, while the next person who enters the room drops one of these coins onto the floor. We then drink a whole mug of ale and tap out. The person who dropped the coin counts, from the time the coin hit the floor until we tap out. The one who drinks the quickest gets to make a demand on the other. The loser can't refuse the demand. Now to be fair the drink has to be clean. We lose one point of count for every drop we spill. Deal?"

Noah smiles meanly. "Done deal, dog basher. Next person to walk in is coin dropper and counter."

They wait while drinking their second ale.

There is a knock and then Seamstress Guilda enters. Both boys smile knowing a seamstress can count. Noah addresses her. "I have a few tasks for you Guilda. You see these stacks on the table. You are going to earn some of the coins. Bloodgrue and I need some clothing as quick as possible. Looking out the window I would say you have three hours to dress Bloodgrue first. But first, Bloodgrue challenged me to a drinking contest. Your part is easy. Drop this Flair I am handing you, onto the floor. Once you hear it hit the floor, start counting. Remember the two numbers when we both tap our mugs on the table. You can stop counting with the tap of the second mug. Got it Sweetheart?"

Guilda smiles as she accepts the coin and she nods. Guilda holds up the coin as the two boys grip the handles of the full mugs. She drops the coin and starts counting at the click of the strike on the floor. Both boys lift their mugs simultaneously. Drinking carefully, but quickly, Noah taps out, quickly followed by Bloodgrue. They smile at each other then look at Guilda. She replies sternly. "Noah 22, Bloodgrue 24. Now let's measure up Bloodgrue. I will go get tunic, legging, vest, belt and boots for you."

Noah smiles happily. "Add a cloak to that as well, a good one. I will have the same set up, thank you Sweetheart."

Guilda sets up Bloodgrue and Noah with a complete set of new clothing each. They eat their hot meal, after they wash up.

Noah turns to Bloodgrue. "Now for my demand, every time you enter Western Madison you have to spend every coin you entered with. Deal?"

Bloodgrue smiles cheerfully and nodding he answers. "Done my friend, I have ten dusters today."

Noah chuckles and pushes a pile of five Flairs to Bloodgrue. "Just spend what you entered with."

To be continued…

In the next episode three, *'Blue Hair and Teptun Square & Market',*

Bloodgrue works the docks bringing clients up to Teptun's Square and Market, dealing with Blue Hair, earning a free chicken carcass.

Awesome! You finished an episode of '*Bloodgrue*'.

Let us know what you think of it by going to this this link: www.inupress.ca While you are there, you can join the Inevitable Unicorn Press e-mail subscription list to receive news and updates about work from our authors such as; Rusty Knight, Brian Hill and Aria. When you sign up for the e-mail list, you will receive a free pdf. This free pdf changes with time. In February 2016 the gift was a copy of Rusty Knight's biography of the protagonists, the Black Swans, from his novel, *'Laret'*. Later in 2016, the bonus would be an issue from the serial series, *'Lanis'*.

While on the home page of InUPress.ca you can leave a comment telling us what you think of our author's work or the website. We appreciate your time and we will respond to questions and comments.

Thank you for reading.

Yours,

Rusty Knight of Inevitable Unicorn Press.

www.inupress.ca

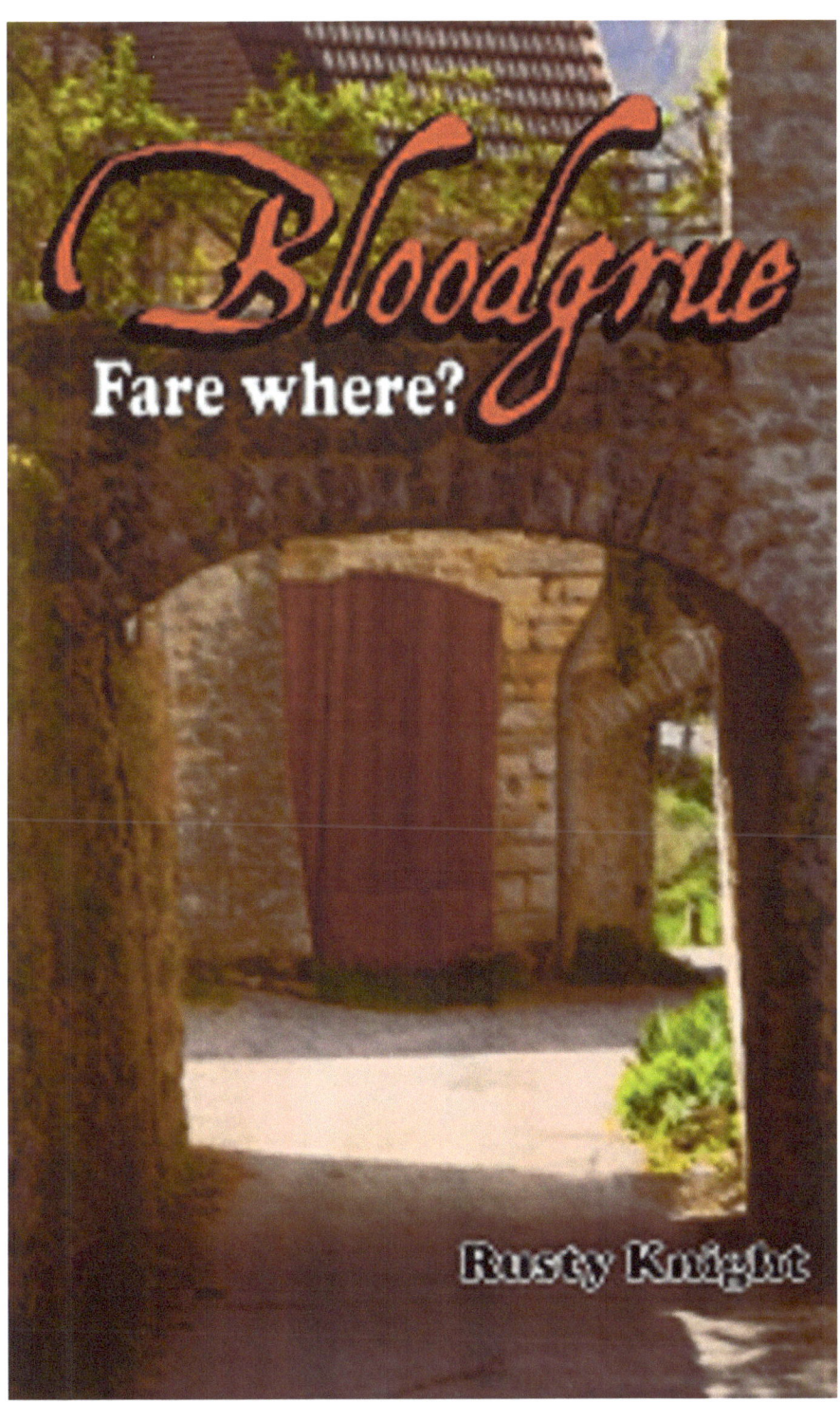

Welcome to our serial stories!

If you're not familiar with our serials, think of them as a favorite nighttime program that continues with a new episode each week, only this is in a print format. These are stories that don't necessarily have an end planned for them, or if they do, it's a long way off unlike many television series that we get interested in, only to have them go off air.

Serial stories are a great way to keep you entertained and on edge waiting to see what will happen next, in short enough episodes to enjoy on a lunch break, or before going to bed. Although our stories are designed to be read one episode per week, unlike TV stories, if you just can't wait for the next episode, you can get another one any time.

Be sure to download your episodes!

It is a good idea to download the episode when you first purchase them. Then, read them at your leisure.

Please feel free to let us know what you think of our serial stories. It's a trend that may take some getting used to, but we've had positive feedback in the past with them.

Now, it's time to enjoy!

Thank you,

From InUPress & Rusty Knight

We would like to acknowledge the following for their work in the production of this series.

The cover design is by, C S Burgar

The editing is by, Donna Shumaker (Aria)

Previously in *Bloodgrue*: ***Autumn 79 Lizard****: Bloodgrue had ventured east into Western Madison to visit his best friend the local peasant hero, Noah. Together they had taken a journey south to meet with a Velan District merchant thug. The thug was intending to purchase Western Madison ward for fifty-five Royal Flairs. Instead, Noah ended up with the gold coins and the thug ended up empty handed.*

Bloodgrue
By Rusty Knight
Episode Three, 'Blue Hair and Teptun Square & Market'

We continue on ...

Autumn 82 Lizard: Bloodgrue just finished escorting a jalnoric family of six to a barge on the docks, for them to sail west to Dendar City on the coast.

Not one to settle for going home light, Bloodgrue is watching for more work as he walks off the docks.

Spotting a lost looking toymal, dripping wet in the drizzle, who is obviously an outter; Bloodgrue sees an opportunity. Approaching the man un-offensively, Bloodgrue speaks to him in toydon. "Good day Master. Are you looking for something?"

The outter, obviously already rattled, hesitates as he cautiously answers. "I could be ... who are you? ... What business is it to you?"

Bloodgrue stands tall and offers his arm to clasp, showing trust. "I am Apprentice Dragoman Bloodgrue, a city guide at your service. Master, I can show you anywhere in the four north districts and a few places farther south."

The outter sighs deeply, but still cautious, he clasps Bloodgrue's arm accepting the universal trust sign. "I am looking for a person, not a place. Can you do that Apprentice Bloodgrue?"

Bloodgrue smiles mischievously. "I know a lot of people. Is it a specific person, or a type of person, you're looking for Master?"

The outter frowns, and then replies with more confidence, as he says. "I am looking for a mine assayer. Do you know one?"

Bloodgrue bows shallowly, and replies with respect. "In Teptun's Square and Market there is a Master Miner Anora. There is him that I know of. If he won't, he will know who will. Will that do?"

The outter stops, looking over Bloodgrue with respect, and he nods happily. "Well yes, that will do. I'm Lander by the way. Sorry, I didn't say before. How long will it take us to get there?"

Bloodgrue looks at Lander's feet and legs, and then he starts walking. After several paces he answers, "I think it will take just over two hours, Master Lander."

The two are almost on Osmo Road, when a call in jalnoric stops Bloodgrue. "Hey Dragoman, hold up a moment."

Bloodgrue looks back, to where he spots a mature toymal hurrying to catch up. Obviously the change into the new clothes has paid off. Bloodgrue hasn't gone one day without a job since Noah supplied the new clothes. In fact, most days he has three or four jobs and this random calling out has become more common place for Bloodgrue.

Waiting for the toymal to catch them, Bloodgrue ponders the reason humorously.

The man, slightly out of breath, stops near Bloodgrue. "I need your help, Apprentice ... The girl in the shop back there ... said you're a reputable dragoman apprentice ... and you know this area ... I am looking for a Master Blue Hair ... Do you know of her?'

Bloodgrue smiles knowingly. "I am going near Blue Hair at this time, come along. It will cost you five dusters."

The man nods, "Done ... five dusters to arrive at Blue Hair." They clasp arms to seal the deal.

Together, the three men walk the hour and a half to Teptun's Square and Market, sorely drenched, wet in the fine mist, as there is no god's breathe moving the droplets one inch in any direction today. It's not thinning out yet it seems. Yes, Bloodgrue knows these conditions don't last long, rarely more than a full day, even in autumn.

Arriving at the north end of the Square, Bloodgrue looks out to the collection of eighty-five stalls and businesses, planning his attack. Blue Hair's stall is 74, in the centre, near the thirty-foot diameter stone fountain. Anora's shop is here in the north-east, at number 80.

With his decision made, Bloodgrue heads for the shop at number 80. Finding the wooden shop, Bloodgrue enters, leading Lander. "Hey there Anora, I have someone here to see you, from out of the city. His name is Lander."

The eighty-one-year-old jalmal turns around from his desk. He looks quizzically at Lander. Anora then snuffles caustically. "Yah, so!"

Lander steps forward to speak, but Bloodgrue stops him with his hand, palm up. "Five dusters Master Lander, then conduct your business with Master Miner Anora."

Lander fishes his coin pouch from its place on his belt. He digs out five copper coins. Placing them on the upheld palm of Bloodgrue, he responds. "Thank you Bloodgrue, where do I find you, if I need you later?"

Bloodgrue places the coins with the rest that are in his coin pouch, while replying. "I will wait by the fountain for another two hours maybe. But my home and its location are three hours from here; you will have difficulty locating me again today. But, if you want me again later, I work from 4212 Willow Road. Find me if you need me, any time I am available. Good day Master Lander and gods-grace, good fate."

Bloodgrue turns next to the other outter. "You know who I am, we didn't introduce you. Before I take you to Blue Hair, you are who?"

The outter frowns and apologizing meekly saying. "My apology, I am Peder of Larden Village. I am a landholder that seeks Blue Hair's services. I know of her by reputation and value her input. She is a known royal information supplier to the outters who come here to Mount Oryn. I need her service."

Bloodgrue nods, as this is very true about Blue Hair.

Bloodgrue walks out of the shop door of number 80. He leads Peder to the centre of the markets. There they find an older blue haired jalfem, hawking butchered chickens. Before approaching, Bloodgrue stops and addresses Peder. "Do you know the protocol, Peder?"

Looking confused, Peder shakes his head. "What protocol? Can't I just ask her what I want to?"

Bloodgrue sighs, having lost count of how many disappointed outters he has witnessed approach Blue Hair. Taking a few moments, Bloodgrue helps this one out. "No. You won't get answers, no matter how simple the question or how common it is, just by walking up and asking her. See those chickens? You're going to have to buy at least one. If you have more than one major question, you need to buy one chicken for each question. Those are your tickets for your questions. You only get as many major questions, as carcasses you buy. It's too bad if she sells out of chickens; you will have to wait until her next market day, for more. Now, if you only have a few minor questions you can get by with one carcass. Prices are important too. Anything about Royalty will cost you at least one Flair per carcass. Nobility questions are roughly, one Flair per carcass. Local, you can usually get by with paying in the range of a few Dyns.

Knowledge has a price Master Peder. Blue Hair has knowledge that is not common. Now you are armed. Don't make mistakes."

Together the two approach stall 74, with Blue Hair and her four remaining wet chicken carcasses. Bloodgrue bows to old Blue Hair. "I have a customer for you once he pays me, Ms. Blue Hair."

Bloodgrue turns to Peder who already has the dusters in hand. Smiling, he gives them to Bloodgrue. "Well worth every one of them, Bloodgrue. Thank you. Wait will you please."

"Master Blue Hair, I seek to purchase one of your chickens. I believe the one I want to be worth five Dyns to me."

Blue Hair nods as she unhooks one of the chickens from its hook. "May I see the Dyns please?"

Peder hands five of his silver coins to Blue Hair, after removing them from his quickly depleting coin purse. Accepting the coins, Blue Hair hands the carcass to Peder. She waits politely for Peder.

Peder takes the chicken and hands it to Bloodgrue. "Wait a while longer Dragoman."

Peder turns attentively to Blue Hair. "I seek to quietly purchase armour, without questioning. Who may I see, Blue Hair?"

Blue Hair sighs deeply; perhaps wondering the legalities of the request, but believing it really none of her business. "How many suits?"

Peder holds up his hand, while extending one finger for Blue Hair. The old woman nods and turns to Bloodgrue. "Take him to Mala, over at stall 12 in the southwest."

"Thank you Blue Hair. I won't forget." Responds Peder positively.

Blue Hair looks him in the eyes while responding sharply. "Please don't."

Bloodgrue nods without responding, other than with a grim grin.

Peder follows Bloodgrue through the crowd. The mists begin breaking up, along with the clouds in the sphere overhead. Stonewire, who shares shedding light with Imvor, begins to shine through the breaks in the cover.

The two men wind their way through stalls, shops and crowds to the far southwestern corner, to stall 12.

Bloodgrue pushes aside the curtain into the large wooden shop. Seeing the nearly half-century old master armour, Bloodgrue approaches the handsome jalmal. Speaking jalnoric Bloodgrue introduces Peder. "Good day Master Mala. I have here an outter, Master Peder, looking for a suit. Once he pays me, I will be on my way to the fountain to wait one hour, if he needs further services from me."

Peder seems to find Mala indifferent, and lowers his arm when no clasping is offered. Then realizing he needs to pay Bloodgrue, Peder unties his coin purse again. "How much Dragoman?"

Bloodgrue decides to take it easy on the man, so he offers. "I will only charge two dusters for this leg, Master Peder. I will wait by the fountain an hour until Stonewire and Imvor reach the top of the tallest western building's peak. Then I will leave for home. You heard, I reside at 4212 Willow Road, if you need me after that."

Bloodgrue accepts the two copper coins from Peder, and then he exits the shop, leaving the two men to their business. He winds his way back through the wet masses, to the centre of the square and stall 74, where he finds Blue Hair packing up her belongings into her hand cart. With no chicken carcasses left hanging from hooks, it means that the business day is over for Blue Hair. She is going home, to 1218 Osmo Road and her six acres of farm land, where she raises her chickens, which she personally butchers each morning for her stall.

Bloodgrue gives Blue Hair a hand, folding down the awning as the process of closing shop continues. "So, do any of your three children visit you any more, Blue Hair? Or, do they only send the grand-children to fetch chickens and coins?"

Blue Hair chuckles, "I still see the youngest occasionally. She brings her brood of five with her to feast every sixth day … and to ask for a tithe, to fend off collectors. But the others keep away, in case my, not so friendly acquaintances … decide to come over calling ... How about you? Your folks call on you yet? How long has it been since you saw them Blood?"

Bloodgrue pauses, and then reaches for his coin pouch, with a smile. "I have several answers for you Blue Hair ... First, as agreed I have a tithe, as for any job you get me outside of Onar's knowledge. I had three Onar jobs today, so he doesn't need to know about Peder going from here to Mala ... I charged two dusters, you are supposed to get ten percent, but I haven't figured out how to legally cut two tenths off a duster, so you keep the whole duster ... Secondly, Mama and Father? … I haven't seen them since they sold me to Master Terep; to be an apprentice dragoman ... I have never seen Arton, my brother since either. So, I have no family, except maybe you ... So it's you and me old one ... Oh, and Noah, over in Western Madison, but if anyone over there heard me say that, I might lose body parts ... Also, maybe include Master Dairius; on one of his good days, as well."

Blue Hair takes the offered duster and tosses it into the coin box with the other gathered Flairs, Dyns and dusters there. She starts pulling her cart through the alleys between stalls. "Go home Bloodgrue ... I don't need youngin. Neither does Dairius ... Keep your focus on your work. That outter won't look for you ... You won't be home until after gods-set now any way. Go home apprentice, another dragoman can tend the outters if they need one tonight."

Bloodgrue sighs sadly. Blue Hair is right about the timing, and he has eleven dusters and seven Dyns in his pouch to tempt the rogues with. *'Yes, time to head home, the outters can tend for themselves. Onar will want me to prepare his evening meal soon.'*

To be continued…

In episode four, *'Dairius'*

Dairius and Bloodgrue help launch a new barge and Bloodgrue orders furniture from the shipyard.

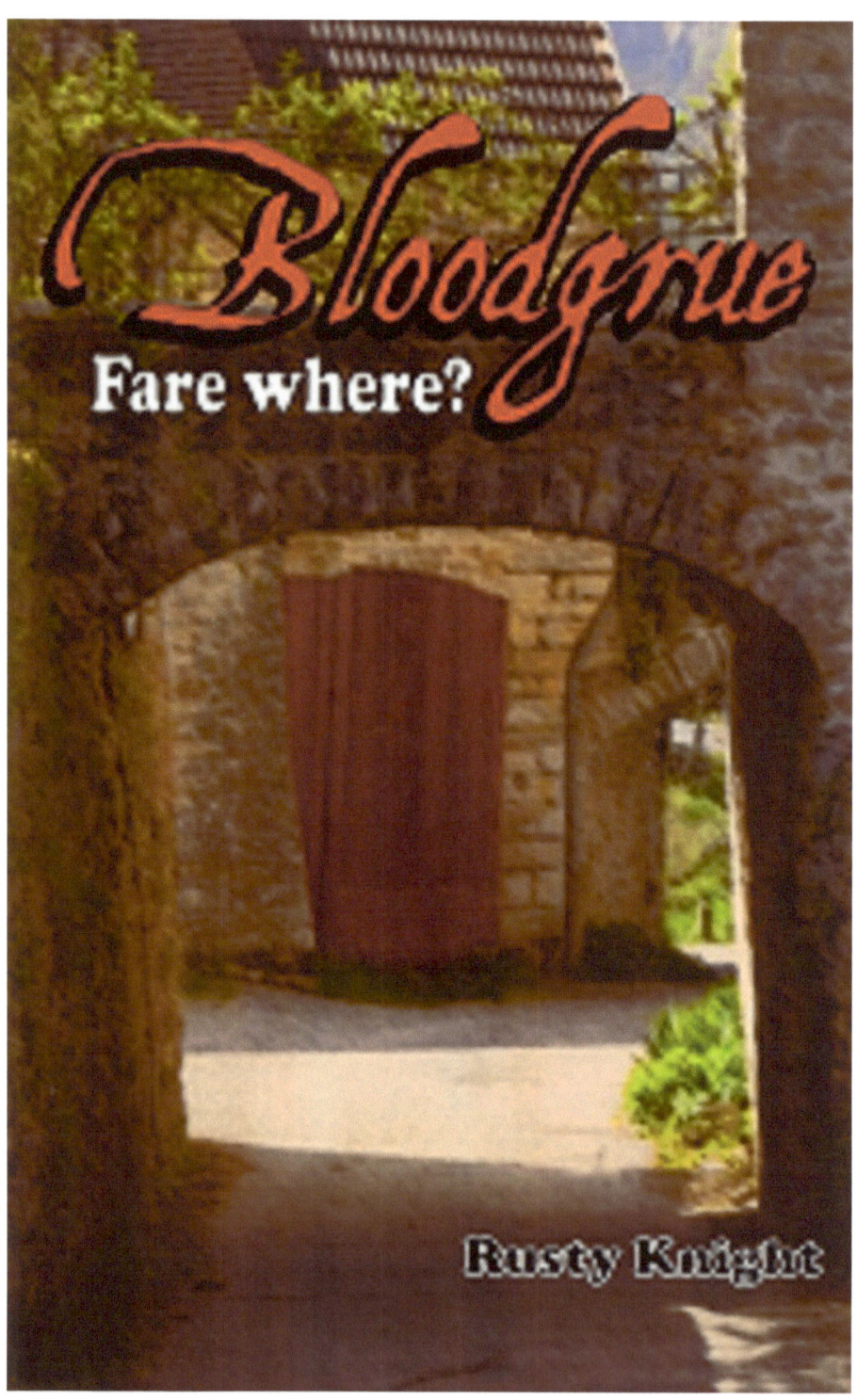

Welcome to our serial stories!

If you're not familiar with our serials, think of them as a favorite nighttime program that continues with a new episode each week, only this is in a print format. These are stories that don't necessarily have an end planned for them, or if they do, it's a long way off unlike many television series that we get interested in, only to have them go off air.

Serial stories are a great way to keep you entertained and on edge waiting to see what will happen next, in short enough episodes to enjoy on a lunch break, or before going to bed. Although our stories are designed to be read one episode per week, unlike TV stories, if you just can't wait for the next episode, you can get another one any time.

Be sure to download your episodes!

It is a good idea to download the episode when you first purchase them. Then, read them at your leisure.

Please feel free to let us know what you think of our serial stories. It's a trend that may take some getting used to, but we've had positive feedback in the past with them.

Now, it's time to enjoy!

Thank you,

From Rusty Knight & InUPress

We would like to acknowledge the following for their work in the production of this series.

The cover design is by, C S Burgar

The editing is by, Donna Shumaker (Aria)

Previously in *Bloodgrue*: ***Autumn 82 Lizard****: Bloodgrue escorted two outters from the docks up to Teptun's Square & Market. Bloodgrue introduced the outter, landholder Lander to Master Miner Anora. Bloodgrue also introduced us to his mentor Blue Hair and her protocol which outters must follow. Bloodgrue pre-warned the outter, Peder, about the proper protocol when dealing with Blue Hair, allowing for a successful transaction and more work for Bloodgrue from a grateful Peder. Bloodgrue also ended up with a free chicken carcass for supper out of the deal.*

Bloodgrue
By Rusty Knight
Episode Four, 'Dairius'

We continue on...

Autumn 87 Lizard: Bloodgrue is down on the docks of the river working with Dairius. Now we could end the story there but we're not going to.

First, let me explain why I haven't told you the name of the river. I could say it simple like, it is because the river doesn't have a name. But that doesn't tell you why. The myth is that once, Royalty angered the gods so fiercely, the gods as a whole decreed that this river should not have a name for one-thousand years. If there should be a name officially put to the river within that one-thousand years, the kingdom will fall to the Shes from the north and from the south, never to rebuild. Mankind would forever be slaves to the Shes kingdoms, to be raised like cattle for their food stock forever and ever. Now, no one wants that fate, so not even the peasants dare put a name to the river. Fortunately, our calendar started on year zero of that curse and the one thousand years is ending at the end of this year. So, next Spring 1, a name can be put to the river, if the count is correct. But last six-day, the Three Councils and Royal Council decreed that to be safe, they would not allow naming of the river for ten more years, to adjust for any slight miscounting. So, the river is simply the river in all its polluted shitty glory.

Dairius is down here at the eastern shipyard dry docks, helping with the launch of a new barge. Dairius has about two years of active duty, he claims, before he will be forced to retire. The old jalmal is ninety-one years old and still slinging freight on and off barges with the best of them. And I mean with the best of them. In the height of his working days he was crew chief doing the work of three men slinging freight with two crews full time.

Enilda Mae never complained, as her life-companion Dairius made enough coin to build the family a two story house, that is theirs, with the title held by them. They stocked away coin for Dairius's retirement and raised Afred and Wilema to be strong healthy adults with their own families.

Dairius though, never satisfied, nestled in with the upper-middle-class folk and became good friends with those who developed into North Docks Council. Now, at Ninety-one, he is semi-retired working on one crew in the shipyard, building and launching new barges for well-to-do customers.

"Bloodgrue, get those fittings secured tighter. This barge is going to let loose with a snap in an hour if all goes well. And Lenila will have my hide if anything pops free. The old jalfem throws fits like none you've ever seen before. So tighten those down tighter." Dairius admonishes Bloodgrue.

The two go over the entire surface of the *'Terry Ada'*, securing every fitting they find as tight as humanly possible. Then, a seventy-some jalfem boards the barge with three others. There are two sailors, a seventy-some jalfem and a half century old toymal. With them is a navigator who Bloodgrue recognizes as Tonal, a half-century old jalmal from Dendar who plies this area of the river frequently.

Tonal, seeing Bloodgrue, laughs and joins him. "SO, Dairius resorted to conniving you into boarding a barge."

Bloodgrue laughs, replying, "It's still on dry ground. There's no water underneath it Master Tonal."

Tonal nods. "Fair enough, for the next half hour. I think you best take to shore now though. We're starting to put water under her soon Blood. You can watch from the dock. Is Dairius paying you fairly?"

Bloodgrue nods. "More than fair and he's feeding me today to top it off. No complaints Master Tonal. I am getting off now."

Bloodgrue walks to the planks to disembark off the *'Terry Ada'* and is greeted by Lenila. "Well apprentice, last chance to get on dry ground. Thank you for helping the old wheezer out. He just won't quit and I don't trust anyone else. You two did well, two days ahead of schedule. There is an extra Dyns in it for you at my office, later."

Bloodgrue bows and offers to clasp arms. Lenila smiles and accepts. As Bloodgrue mounts the planks, both sailors snarl insults at Bloodgrue in unkind sailor jargon. "You couldn't swab my spittle off the brass monkey, boy. Get off our barge." says the toymal sarcastically.

The jalfem takes a kick at Bloodgrue as she swears. "Damn landy, couldn't walk ten minutes on the river in winds. Get outta here, back to your mamma's tits."

Bloodgrue ignores both of them, not acknowledging either of them.

Up on the solid dock; Bloodgrue watches as Lenila begins removing the barrier's planking that is holding back the water from the dry cell. Water starts to wash in the rubble and soil, and then fill the cell. Slowly the cell fills with water and the sailors remove the remaining wall planks from the barrier. Bloodgrue watches the dirt and rubble rush in, washed down by the water. The *'Terry Ada'* rises with the rising water level. There is steady popping with the flexing of her timbers adjusting. Lenila, Dairius and the two sailors stand on her deck watching around them. Bloodgrue watches anxiously, anticipating any possible fixture popping free. After two hours, the water and the *'Terry Ada'* have settled. The four on board inspect the entire barge, and then after holding a meeting they clasp arms.

Exiting the barge last, Dairius comes over to Bloodgrue with a grim expression. "She's not going to pay me, so I can't pay you, Blood. Sorry lad. You're going home empty handed and empty bellied."

Bloodgrue looks at Dairius in disbelief. He just saw celebration, not dissatisfaction, and then he sees the telltale twinkle in his friend's eyes. Smiling, he asks sarcastically. "Where are we eating? Is Enilda cooking for us? I like the bread she cooks."

Dairius bursts out laughing and extends his arm. Bloodgrue clasps arms with Dairius, waiting for a reply.

Done clasping arms, Dairius pulls free his coin purse. "I made you a couple promises and I am going to add to them. You did great work these two days Bloodgrue. Lenila was impressed with us. So she's paying a bonus. Here are your two Dyns pay. You get to eat my life-companions cooking for evening meal. Plus, I recall how you said you have no furniture in your room. Master Onar has not supplied any. You have a few rare coins burning holes in your coin pouch. I have a few extra as well; let's go see if we can remedy this situation. Deal?"

Bloodgrue stops in his tracks. He had never considered buying himself furniture, or anything for that matter. And yes, he does have five Flairs in his pouch;

he forgot he mentioned them to Dairius and Blue Hair. "Okay, where to?"

"How about our master woodworker; from the barge? She's not busy now." suggests a twinkling eyed Dairius. He leads Bloodgrue to the group of buildings next to the dry dock cell.

They enter the woodworking shop to find an octogenarian jalfem organizing the tools. Dairius approaches her boldly. "Enna, are you available for a few small projects, or are some of your apprentices?"

The jalfem turns, scowling. "You old goat, why would I help you after the last ruse you pulled on my new journeyman?"

Dairius laughs. "I paid you double for that. This isn't for me and it's serious. It's for the apprentice dragoman. He is in need of some furniture. You can assign it to your younger journeymen if you want. It's not a favour to me. It's a paying job for a customer. What do you say?"

Enna walks over to Bloodgrue, looking him over she asks gruffly. "What do you have to say, boy?"

Bloodgrue stands confidently, knowing he's being addressed as a customer. "I am here to purchase some items to have built for me. Three items I think."

Enna nods and continues straight on. "Okay, what's your name and tell me what you want. I'll decide who I assign the work to and the cost to you."

Bloodgrue smiles, as he enjoys this part of any conversation. "I am Apprentice Dragoman Bloodgrue of 4212 Willow Road. What I want is a single bed, a dresser and a small table. Come to think of it, I might be able to add a simple chair in my room as well. I would like it delivered when it is ready."

Enna smiles approvingly. "I like you; you have an idea already what you want, and you're not trying to guess or decide now. So I will make it easy, I know which journeyman and apprentice will work on this. The bed I want five Dyns for, the dresser seven Dyns. A small table of say … three feet to a side will be about … four Dyns I am thinking. We will do the chair for … oh … four Dyns as well. Can you afford that apprentice?"

Bloodgrue hesitates, and then shakes his head. "Not good enough. I want a fancier bed and chair. Fancy enough the works will be worth three Flairs."

Enna looks at Dairius quizzically, then back to Bloodgrue. "I will do that, but you have to get your own mattress and pillows."

Bloodgrue extends his arm, smiling gleefully.

Enna shrugs and says sternly. "If we clasp, it seals the deal and you owe me three Flairs one way or another."

Bloodgrue keeps his arm up. So Enna clasps grimly.

Bloodgrue pulls free his coin pouch, empties out three Flairs and hands them to Enna who is looking confused, then shocked, as does Dairius who hadn't really taken Bloodgrue serious to be carrying the coins with him here.

"How soon can I expect delivery, Master Enna?" asks a smirking Bloodgrue.

Enna stashes the coins in her coin box, and then thinking, she answers. "4212 Willow road? I think we can have these over there by Winter 10. I will divide it up into two teams to ensure that."

Bloodgrue, smiling, asks. "Is there a seamstress here I can purchase the mattress and pillows from?

Enna turns to Bloodgrue, thinking a moment, and then she replies. "There are two. Master Lar Tol, an old toymal who is grumpier then me and is the same age. You want the younger tailor, the jalmal in building three. His name is Menald, just say I recommended him to you. He did the sails and cloth work for the *Terry Ada*."

Dairius and Bloodgrue bow then exit.

Arriving at building three, they enter and look around. Bloodgrue spots a jalmal stitching a new sheet. "Gods-grace, good fate, master. Are you Menald?" asks Bloodgrue cautiously.

The jalmal puts down his work. Blurry eyed, he looks towards Bloodgrue. "Yes I am. What might I do for you?"

"I am Apprentice Dragoman Bloodgrue. Master Woodworker Enna said you are the one to see for some items I wish to purchase. Do you have time to talk now?"

Menald stands and walks over to the desk to join his two guests. "Of course, I just finished up with the *Terry Ada* and was getting a start on a new barge's gear. Tell me what I can do for you?"

Bloodgrue smiles disarmingly. "I seek to have a single-size feather mattress, and a feather pillow made and delivered to 4212 Willow Road, by Winter 10."

Menald chuckles as he replies. "I have each already in stock. For one Flair they will be delivered by tomorrow gods-set."

Bloodgrue extends his arm, and nearly shouts. "Done and what about two blankets to go with them?"

Menald answers by clasping arms and offering. "I stock wool blankets at two Dyns a piece. How many do you want me to send?"

Bloodgrue pulls free his coin pouch with its two Flairs and two Dyns. Making a quick decision, he answers. "I made my mind up, just one. Here are your Flair and two Dyns. Good fates and god's grace. Thank you."

Bloodgrue leaves the shop with one Royal Flair in his coin pouch and his loyal friend by his side.

Together, the two walk the three hours to 3212 Monrose Road, Dairius's home. The two story twenty-foot by thirty-foot house was built for Dairius's family forty-seven years ago. It stands beautifully tall and sturdy.

Entering, one finds a clean, neat, orderly interior. The smell of fresh baked bread overwhelms Bloodgrue. "Can I come in and eat?"

Dairius's instantly replies. "NO."

But then he chortles violently for a minute or so while waving Bloodgrue in.

Enilda, hearing Dairius teasing someone again, comes to see who this victim is. Seeing Bloodgrue, she smiles. "Come in Blood. You're staying for evening meal of course? You are looking good. I like your new clothes. When did you get those? Dairius never mentioned them."

"Hello Master Enilda. I just received them a few days ago. Thank you for noticing. I think Dairius missed them. He helped me a lot today, so I forgive him. You were baking today; I can smell it. I look forward to tasting the delights you cooked up."

Dairius, feeling left out, adds. "Blood worked hard today so he gets two helpings. But not my size of helpings, same size as Afred's. Let's get in there and eat; I'm hungry."

So goes another day for Bloodgrue…

To be continued…

In episode five, *'North Docks'*

We walk with Bloodgrue starting in Anchor's Rest, then on his return home he escorts a wayward sailor home to Morelot Morring where he picks up a package to go to Low Tide, there he picks up rare salvage.

Bloodgrue serial series will be continued in *Bloodgrue* Volume 2, Breaths, with Episodes 5 through 10.

© 2016 Rusty Knight with Inevitable Unicorn Press

www.inupress.ca rusty@inupress.ca

Our follow-up *Bloodgrue* Volumes are available on Kindle and paperback on Amazon, as well *Bloodgrue* Volume 3, Business is also available as e-book on InUPress and Kobo.

- *Bloodgrue* Volume 2, Breaths
- *Bloodgrue* Volume 3, Business

Coming up on InUpress, Amazon, Kindle and Kobo next is:

- *Bloodgrue* Volume 4, Attraction

Check-out Dalan e-zine while you're at InUPress as well.

Awesome! You finished an episode of '*Bloodgrue*'.

Let us know what you think of it by going to this this link: www.inupress.ca While you are there, you can join the Inevitable Unicorn Press e-mail subscription list to receive news and updates about work from our authors such as; Rusty Knight, Brian Hill and Aria. When you sign up for the e-mail list, you will receive a free pdf. This free pdf changes with time. In February 2016 the gift was a copy of *Rusty Knight's* biography of the protagonists, the Black Swans, from his novel, *'Laret'*. Later in 2016, the bonus was an issue from the serial series, *'Lanis'*.

While on the home page of InUPress.ca you can leave a comment telling us what you think of our author's work or your thought about the website. We appreciate your time and we will respond to questions and comments.

Thank you for reading.

Yours,

Rusty Knight of Inevitable Unicorn Press.

www.inupress.ca